THE SHOP

Carol Watson
Illustrated by Colin King

Series Editor: Heather Amery
Consultant: Betty Root

We go to the store

awning

window

jars

bag

cake

bottles

storekeeper

basket

newspaper
stand

carriage

dog

It has

two big windows,

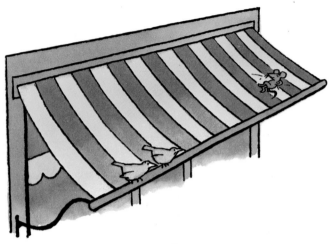

a striped awning,

a newspaper stand,

and a storekeeper.

3

Inside the store

shelf

window

scales

storekeeper

knife

counter

cashier

cash register

check-out

cart

4

BREAD AND CAKES

cake

can

bottle

bread

basket

packages

freezer

box

barrel

tube

5

Mom wants

a wire basket,

and a big cart.

We look at bottles

SOFT DRINKS

and cans.

We take

a box off the shelf,

peas from the freezer,

apples from the barrel

and a bag of sugar.

We look at the meat and fish.

MEAT and FISH

sausages

ham

fish

knife

paper

chicken

steaks

bacon

We buy

five steaks,

two big fish,

some sausages

and a fat chicken.

Mom buys vegetables and fruit.

FRUIT

peaches

mushrooms

plant

pumpkin

scales

potatoes

carrots

melon

bananas

We pick up

a bunch of bananas,

a box of mushrooms,

a bag of onions

and two heads of lettuce.

The man weighs

some apples

and lots of carrots.

He drops a cabbage

and steps on a tomato.

We find the bread and cakes.

BREAD AND CAKES

icing

fruit cake cake

chocolate cake

rolls

loaf

doughnuts

bread

cookie

roll

We take ten rolls,

two loaves of bread,

a package of cookies,

and a chocolate cake.

We stop at the dairy counter

DAIRY FOODS

milk

margarine

butter

cheese

cream

yogurt

eggs

We buy

six cups of yogurt,

two cartons of eggs,

three cartons of milk

and some cheese.

We find lots of things to read.

Books and Magazines

books

pens

newspaper

pencil

magazine

baby

candy

hand bag

comic

Mom stops to talk to her friends.

We want

some new pencils,

colored pens

and some candy and chocolate for Dad.

At last we have finished.

Mom opens her purse and drops all her money.

We pay the cashier,

fill up the bags
and off we go.

Here is a puzzle.
Mom put these things into her bag.

cake

carrots

bananas

chicken

fish

cheese

eggs

sausages

lettuce

Can you see what she lost on the way home?

Here is another puzzle

Can you find a bottle, a jar, a cake, some bread and a bag of onions?

First published in 1980
by Usborne Publishing Ltd
20 Garrick Street
London WC2 9BJ, England
© Usborne Publishing Ltd 1980

Printed in Belgium

The name Usborne and the device ⊕ are
Trade Marks of Usborne Publishing Ltd.